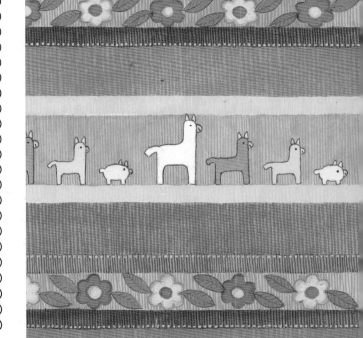

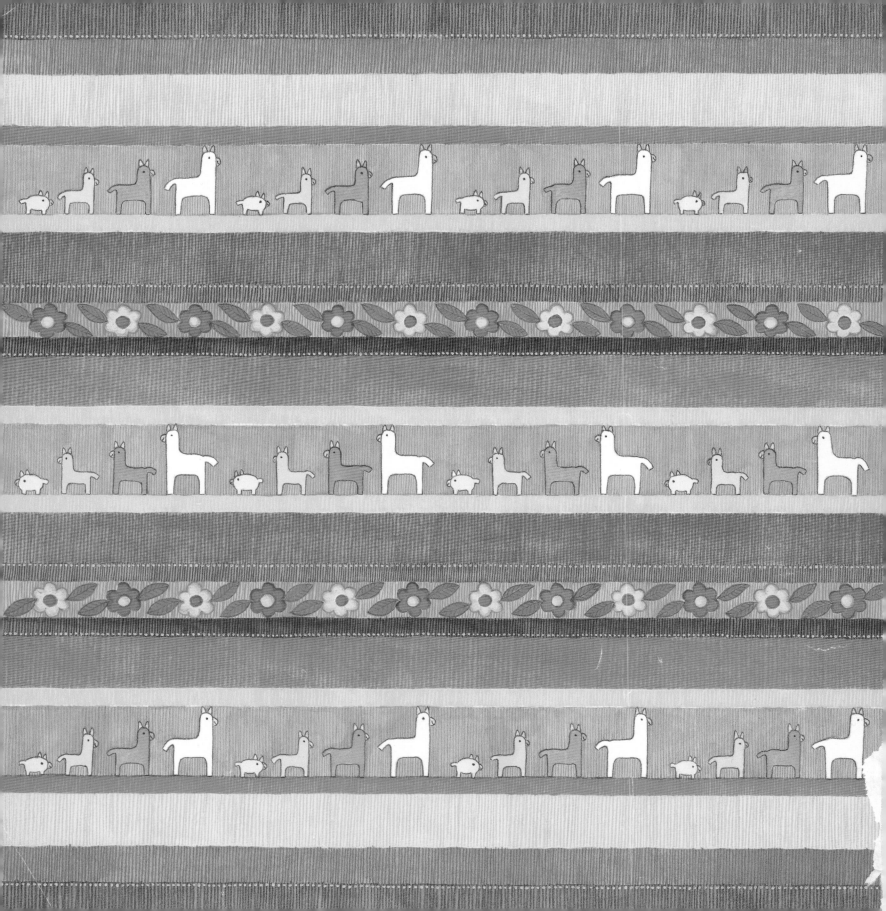

A Stack of Alpacas

MATT COSGROVE

Scholastic Press • New York

For Madeleine and John,
my niece and nephew
(who are nothing at all like Reece, Roo, and Drew)
— M.C.

Library of Congress Cataloging-in-Publication Data available

ISBN 978-1-338-71622-1

10 9 8 7 6 5 4 3 2 1   20 21 22 23 24

Printed in China 38
This edition first printing, October 2020

The type was set in Mr Dodo featuring Festivo LC.

This guy is called **Macca.**

He's an alpaca!

He collects **funny caps,**

and **loves**
to take
NAPS!

That guy is called
Drew.

He's Macca's nephew!

He's round as a **bubble** and ...

Here are Macca's nieces. He loves them to pieces.

They're called
Reece and **Roo**,

and they're trouble *TIMES TWO!*

"STACKS ON Uncle Mac!"

CRACK!

"Oh, my back!"

When the trio came to stay, they played all day,
and thought it was cool to break every rule.

RULES
- eat your veggies
- play nicely
- use your manners
- be tidy
- act sensibly

They **fought** over toys

and made lots of **noise.**

VROOM!

BOOM!

There was **SMASHING** and splashing!

FIGHTING and biting!

Zoning...

...then **moaning.**

Macca looked at the mess
and **CRACKED**
from the stress!

"**Reece, Roo,** and **Drew,**
I expect more from you!"

Seeing Uncle Mac
completely **blow his stack,**
the trio was surprised . . .

After they **cuddled**, the alpacas all **huddled**,
and came up with a plan to get things
spick — and — **span.**

From high to low
it was **go!**

Go!

Go!

Reece **rubbed**
and **wiped.**

Roo **scrubbed**
and **swiped.**

Drew **dusted**
and **scooped...**

...until they were all
POOPED!

"**I'm so proud of you three,**"
Macca whispered softly.

But as he left them to sleep,
he accidentally went . . .

BEEP!

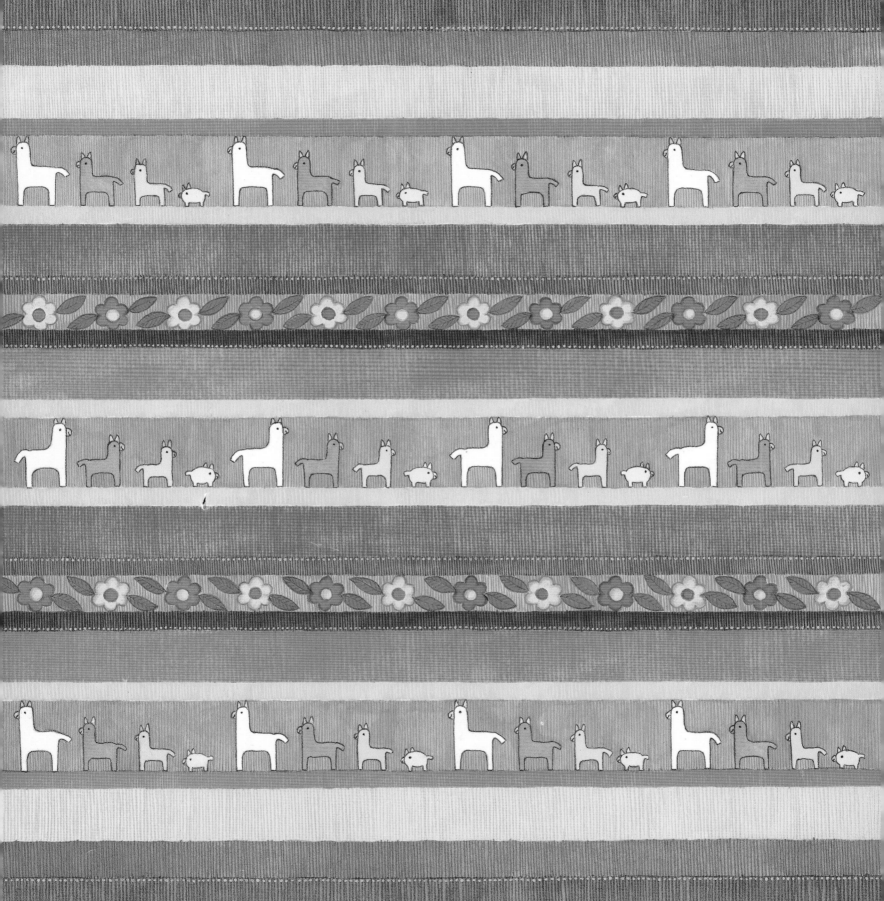

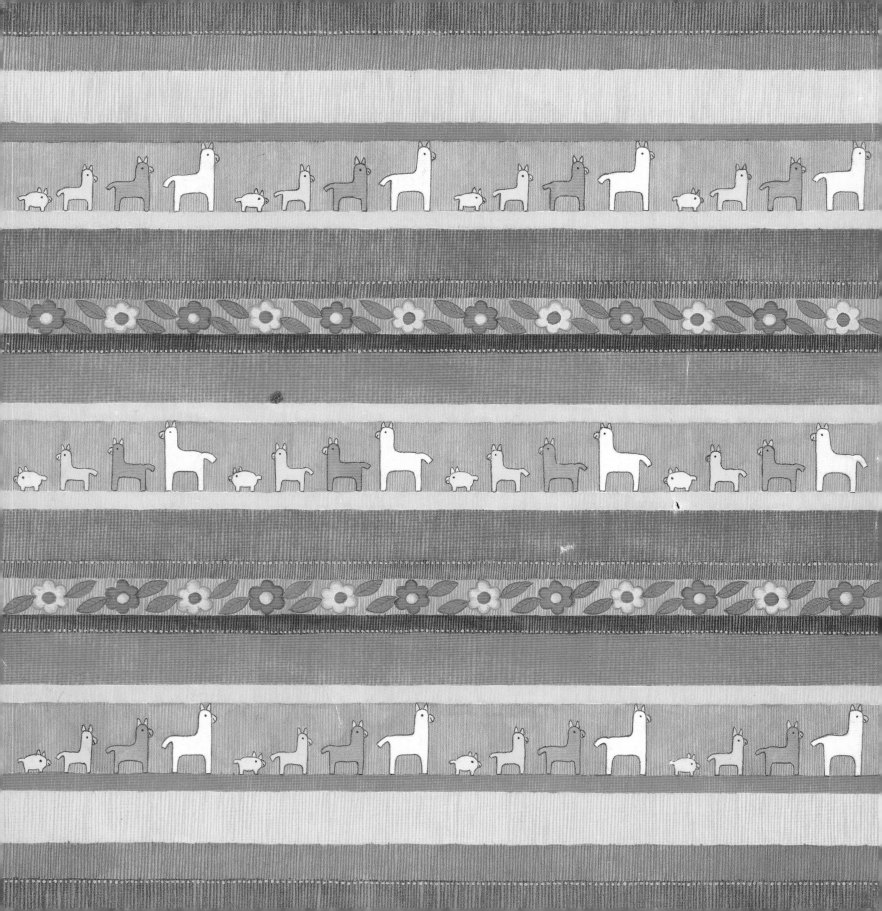

© for the French edition: L'Élan vert, Saint-Pierre-des-Corps, 2019
Title of the original edition: La petite Danseuse
© for the English edition: Prestel Verlag, Munich · London · New York, 2020
A member of Verlagsgruppe Random House GmbH
Neumarkter Strasse 28 · 81673 Munich

Library of Congress Control Number: 2019953591
A CIP catalogue record for this book is available from the British Library.

Translated from the French by Paul Kelly
Copyediting: Brad Finger
Project management: Melanie Schöni
Production management and typesetting: Susanne Hermann
Printing and binding: TBB, a.s.

Verlagsgruppe Random House FSC® N001967

Prestel Publishing compensates the CO_2 emissions produced from
the making of this book by supporting a reforestation project in Brazil.
Find further information on the project here:
www.ClimatePartner.com/14044-1912-1001

Printed in Slovakia
ISBN 978-3-7913-7449-9
www.prestel.com

Géraldine Elschner – Olivier Desvaux

The Little
DANCER

A Children's Book Inspired by
Edgar Degas

PRESTEL

Munich · London · New York

With her hair flowing in the wind, Jeanne is spellbound by Paris.
She gazes at the Pont de Flandre lock and the Saint-Martin canal…
the carriage rumbling along the cobblestones.
The towers of Notre-Dame appear in the distance, and beyond them
the Grands Boulevards. What a world! What bustle!
Suddenly, Clémence grabs her daughter's hand.
"Jeanne, look!," she exclaims.
In front of them stand golden wings glistening in the sun.
It's the Opera Garnier; they have arrived.

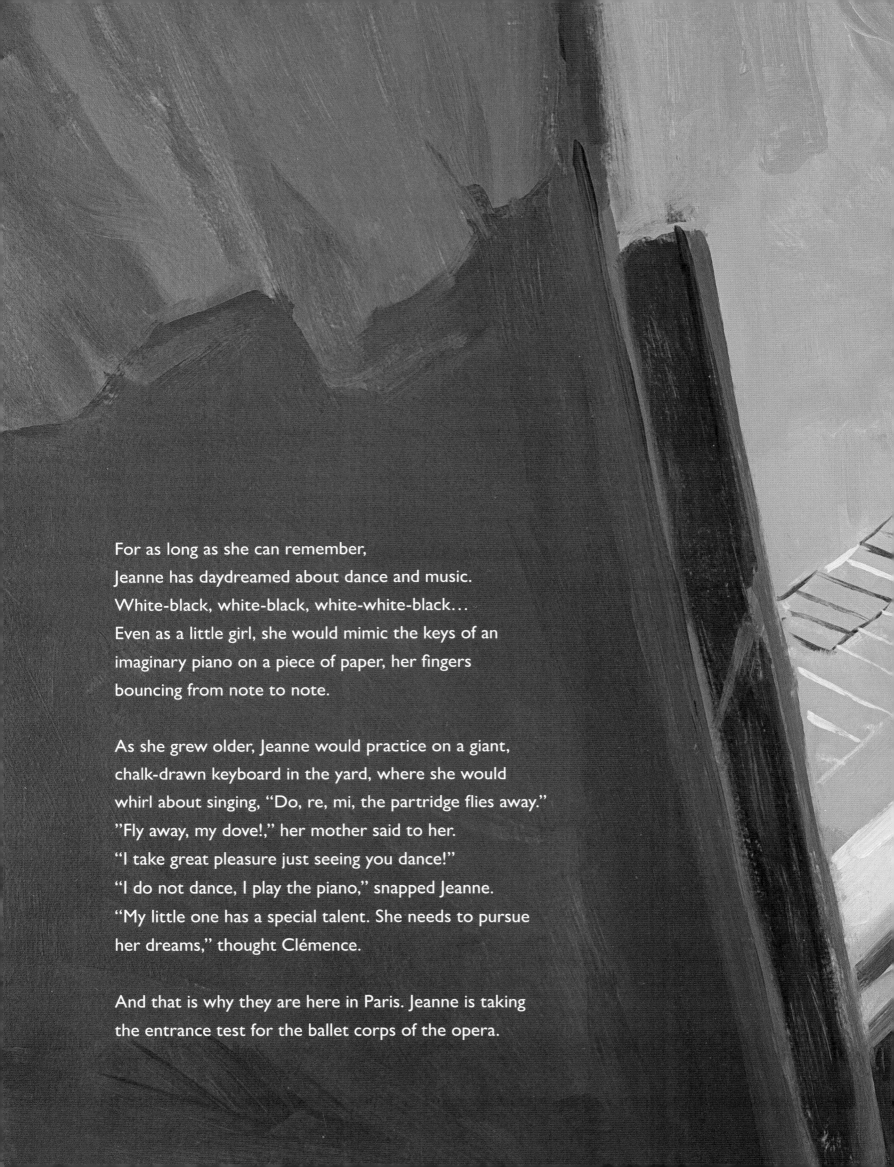

For as long as she can remember,
Jeanne has daydreamed about dance and music.
White-black, white-black, white-white-black…
Even as a little girl, she would mimic the keys of an
imaginary piano on a piece of paper, her fingers
bouncing from note to note.

As she grew older, Jeanne would practice on a giant,
chalk-drawn keyboard in the yard, where she would
whirl about singing, "Do, re, mi, the partridge flies away."
"Fly away, my dove!," her mother said to her.
"I take great pleasure just seeing you dance!"
"I do not dance, I play the piano," snapped Jeanne.
"My little one has a special talent. She needs to pursue
her dreams," thought Clémence.

And that is why they are here in Paris. Jeanne is taking
the entrance test for the ballet corps of the opera.

Clémence paces up and down outside the rehearsal room.
Will her daughter be accepted? The exam is very difficult!
Inside the room, Jeanne skips lightly on the floorboards,
which look a lot like the keyboard of a piano.
The wait that follows seems endless. Yet when the results are announced,
both mother and daughter are filled with joy. Success! She's done it!

A new life begins — a place to live, a tiny
apartment in Montmartre, a job in the laundry house
for Clémence and the opera for Jeanne.

The days are not easy, however.
Dance classes, rehearsals, performances…
From morning to evening, Jeanne performs
her exhausting workouts with the other 'little brats'
of the ballet corps. None of the girls ever evade
the eyes of Mademoiselle Dihau, who sits at the piano
and puts them through their paces.

The two francs earned each day are welcome. 2 + 2 + 2…
And at night, Jeanne dreams of a piano that dances.
Her feet are bruised, her legs are painful, but despite everything
she never loses sight of her goal.

While the little brats practice tirelessly, a man is working near them.
He observes them for hours, capturing every gesture,
every moment, and then refining every movement.
His charcoal drawings come alive. How beautiful all of these dancers
become through his pencil!

One day, the man approaches Jeanne. She may not have the elegance of her fellow dancers, but her rhythmic pace makes her stand out from the rest.

"Young Marie, who is modelling for me, has fallen ill," he says.

"Would you agree to stand in for her?"

Jeanne does not hesitate. That will earn her a few extra francs. And she is curious to see 'Monsieur D.' at work.

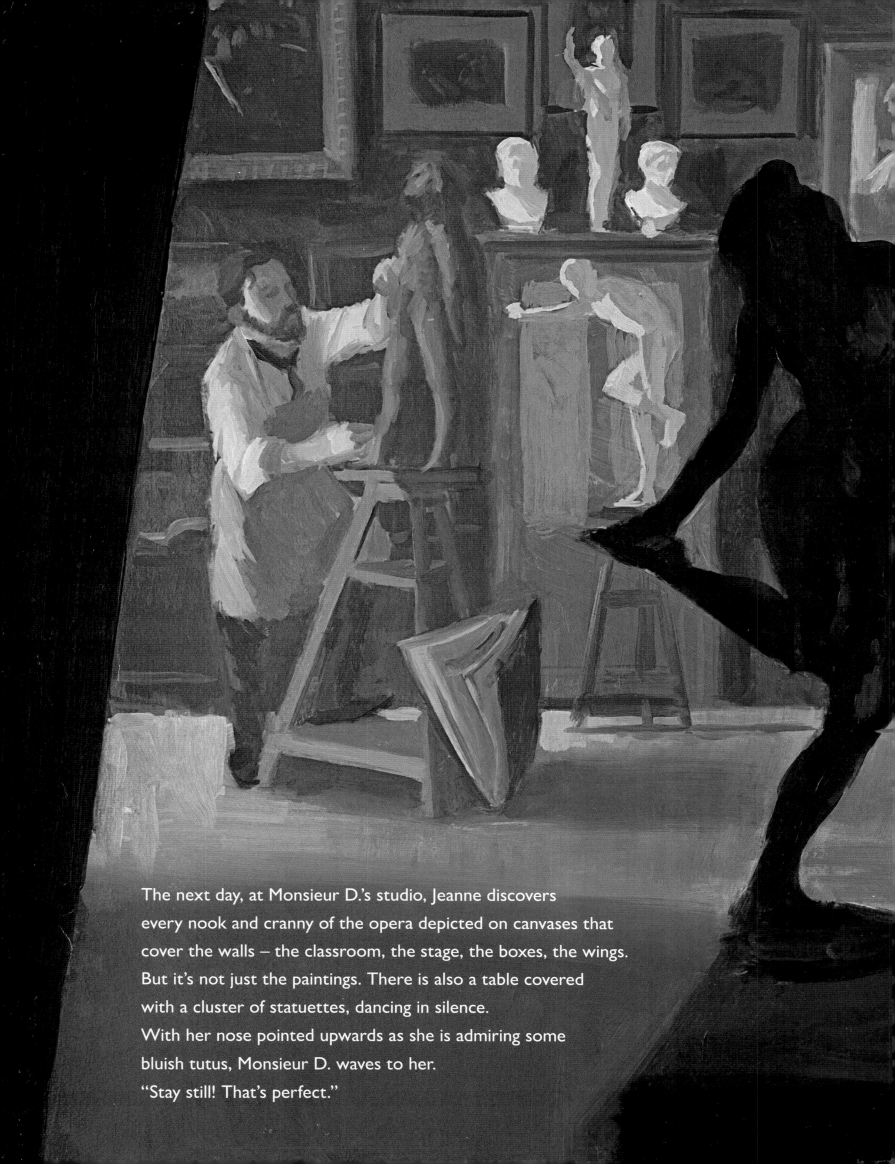

The next day, at Monsieur D.'s studio, Jeanne discovers
every nook and cranny of the opera depicted on canvases that
cover the walls – the classroom, the stage, the boxes, the wings.
But it's not just the paintings. There is also a table covered
with a cluster of statuettes, dancing in silence.
With her nose pointed upwards as she is admiring some
bluish tutus, Monsieur D. waves to her.
"Stay still! That's perfect."

With her hands behind her back and a casual look on her face,
Jeanne often gets the butterflies in Monsieur D.'s studio.
Yet, she untiringly recovers, ties a ribbon through her hair,
and holds her pose.
With each position, the artist uses his fingers to transform
his wax model, his little dancer.
But who does it resemble? Marie? Jeanne?
It has the appearance of one, yet the posture of the other.
A kind of Marie-Jeanne…

There are great preparations for the end-of-the-year show
at the opera: one, two, three – leaps, pirouettes,
folds, entrechat, arabesques. Jeanne tries harder than ever.
That evening, she can hardly feel her feet, back, or neck.
She thinks of giving up a thousand times. And a thousand times,
she starts all over again.
Oh, what an easier life she has, that wax sister of hers!

Finally, one evening, Jeanne puts on her festive costume.
Her hands are trembling and her heart pounding.
At the moment the orchestra strikes up for a tremendous ballet,
a cloud of tutus enters the stage.
The dancers twirl about to the music in a rustle of frilled fabric.
Sitting up in her box, Clémence has tears in her eyes.

At the end of the show, there is an energy in the wings.

"Well done, my dove! One day, you will be a star dancer,"
exclaims Clémence.

"Me, a star?," jokes Jeanne. "It takes more than dancers to make a ballet.
You need music to blend with the movement."

"In that case, learn how to play the piano," says Monsieur D.
"You would make a good choreographer, too! But at this stage,
let us celebrate your first success — as well as that of my little dancer!
I have just finished it."

"Really? Can I go and see her?," pleads Jeanne.
"By all means. And to help you pay for your music lessons,
you are always welcome as a model in my studio –
both you and Marie, of course!"

Jeanne arrives at the studio the next day.
With heartfelt emotion, she greets her double.
And then she hands Monsieur D. a small,
ribbon-tied package that he recognizes immediately.
Within the flower-printed paper, he finds Jeanne's
first tutu and her slippers.
"They are too small for me now," she says.
"But I know who would be able to wear them."

The artist burst out laughing.
"Come on! Let's dress our little dancer
without further ado. And one day,
you will tell us her story … at the opera!"

EDGAR DEGAS

The Little Fourteen-Year-Old Dancer

1922 (cast), 2018 (tutu), partially tinted bronze,
cotton tarlatan, silk satin, and wood,

38.5 inches (97.8 cm), The Metropolitan Museum of Art, New York,

H. O. Havemeyer Collection, Bequest of Mrs. H. O. Havemeyer, 1929

The original wax sculpture is in the National Gallery of Art
in Washington D.C. but a limited number of casts of this sculpture
can be found in famous museums around the world such as
the Tate, London, and Musée d'Orsay, Paris.

EDGAR DEGAS

ID CARD

NAME: Degas
FIRST NAME: Edgar
1834 – 1917
Painter, sculptor, engraver, and photographer
STYLE: Impressionism and Realism

A TRUE STORY

Behind the tale in this book lies a very real story, namely that of Marie van Goethem, who modelled for Edgar Degas. The daughter of a laundress, she was born in one of the poorest neighborhoods of Paris in 1865. Young Marie and her two sisters were admitted as dance students at the Paris opera by 1878. One day, when Marie was on stage, Degas saw her from the audience and became fascinated. He asked her if she would pose for him as a model. And so Marie was able to earn a few extra francs by modelling for Degas. She had been hired at the opera for a meager salary as a 'walk-on' – a member of the ballet corps who danced almost hidden at the back of the stage. Marie would later be dismissed from the opera for missing too many dance classes…

A DIFFICULT APPRENTICESHIP

We like to remember Marie van Goethem and the other 'walk-ons' as aspiring star dancers. But the reality is much more sordid. Poor families at that time sacrificed their daughters to the opera, especially because the dance classes given there were provided free of charge, as were the outfits (slippers, leotards, etc.). And let's not forget that child labor was commonplace at the time and represented a valuable extra income for needy parents. *Little Dancer Aged Fourteen* symbolizes, therefore, a difficult life – the life of the 'little brats' of the opera, who exhausted their bodies to provide entertainment for wealthy Parisians.

AN OBJECT OF SCANDAL

The sculpture depicts a young ballerina. She stands in a state of rest, her legs apart, hands behind her back, chest out, head thrown backwards, and her feet forming the classical fourth position. She is dressed in a silk bustier, a frilled tutu, stockings, and dance slippers. Her hair is tied in a satin ribbon.

The original sculpture, in colored wax to imitate the hue of real skin, was modelled around a structure of paint brushes, wires, and other materials. Degas then fitted his wax girl with real fabric accessories and a proper wig. During its exhibition in 1881, the sculpture caused shock and scandal because of the technique used and its realism. Some even thought there was something cruel about the work. Other observers, however, regarded the sculpture as a particularly novel attempt at modern art. Today, we can see *The Little Fourteen-Year-Old Dancer* as a moving testimony by Degas, one that has enabled this young girl to transcend time and be seen by future generations.

DID DEGAS ONLY PAINT DANCERS?

No… even though he received the nickname 'painter of the dancers.' Degas did spent a lot of time with ballerinas. He liked to watch their daily workout. Unlike high society women who were stuck in their rigid clothes and boots, the dancers were agile and graceful, able to perform all kinds of steps, to lift their legs, to jump, and to spin. They were an inexhaustible subject of observation for the painter. Degas faithfully reproduced their postures not only during their exercises, but also while they were at rest. However, he wasn't interested in dancers alone. Degas also expressed his fascination for natural movement in other subjects: laundresses, bathing women, and even racehorses!